For the love of Elizabeth, daughter my moon.

Oh! The Things You Can See In The Dark!

story and pictures by Cathleen Francisco

Special thanks to

Dr. Timothy Blair
Professor of Reading Education UCF
and founder of
Saturday Reading Camp, Orlando, FL

Luna Michelis
for bringing light to the idea

Oh! The Things You Can See In The Dark! is a picture book for children ages 3 and up with the focus being on the illustrations versus storyline. The premise of the book is to reveal that which can only be seen in the dark or those things made more glorious by the absence of light. While children may often perceive the dark to be ominous, this book shows a magical aspect of the night through the imagery used. There may be a note of tension in a storm cloud or a rolling sea, but the components of the images are familiar to children and the scene is ultimately quieting, curious and inviting. Showing the dark as a place of discovery offers an opportunity for parents to engage a child about the wonder and beauty of the night.

The text is divided between child and adult. For the child, simple questions that can lead to curious discoveries. For the adult, a bit of trivia to offer a stepping off place for the reader to begin a dialogue with the child, create a story of their own, or continue to explore the night.

The coat of the red fox can vary, but it is the white-tipped tail that makes them easy to identify. Foxes are very social animals, living in a family group with a dominate mated pair. On average, four to six kits are born in spring and pack members help raise and care for them.

They live in the open but will burrow in winter, often sharing their den with other animals like badgers and woodchucks. You will see them primarily at night, however, they are not strictly nocturnal and will also hunt at dawn and dusk. The red fox is a carnivore, but its diet also includes plants and fruit. Blueberries, blackberries, raspberries, cherries, apples, plums, and grapes are some of their favorites.

Half of the moon is always lit by the sun, the other half stays in darkness. As the moon orbits the earth we see changes in the moon's illumination. This is referred to as the moon's phases. Changes in the moon's appearance are due to the positions of the moon and the sun in relation to (with) the earth. The phases are not caused by the earth's shadow; rather it is our perspective and the angle at which we see the moon's illuminated side. At certain times we see a combination of the moon's shadowed side as well as the sunlit portion, creating some of the phases we recognize in the night sky.

Eight phases occur each lunar month - every 29.5 days as the moon makes its revolution around the earth. We don't see the new moon because its illuminated side faces away from the earth. The full moon and the two half moons are easy to identify in the night sky. The four phases between them - gibbous, crescent, waxing and waning - add further distinction to the lunar profile. When the earth casts its shadow on the moon, we experience a lunar eclipse.

PHASES OF THE MOON

In the darkness of night,
the moon shines bright.
What does the moon look like tonight?
Did you know the moon has eight different names?
How many names do you have?

A pond is a small, still, shallow body of water. Because it lacks a current, the pond's calm nature is ideal for many forms of life to thrive. Most frog species spend life near water; in a pond, river bank, quiet stream, or even puddle. There they lay eggs from which tadpoles, or polliwogs, are born. Depending on the species a tadpole can take anywhere from a few months to years to fully develop into a frog. Pond life, while it has its dangers, is an amiable ecosystem in which our polliwog friends can mature. Once these amphibians have morphed into their second life as frogs, they tend to stay near a water source. Some even migrate, returning to the same pond they were born in to lay their offspring.

It is vital that a frog's skin remain moist, as it is one of the ways they breath. Not all frogs are nocturnal, but the ones that are use the humidity and cool night temperatures to help retain moisture. Frogs do not drink water but absorb it through their skin which makes them more susceptible to the toxins in the water. Insects, a major part of the frog's diet, are in abundance at night and the frogs take full advantage, sitting perfectly still as they wait for dinner to come their way.

THE POND

In the darkness of night,
the quiet pond comes to life and the frogs begin their croaking.
Can you sound like a frog?
What colors, besides brown, can frogs be?
Can you find the blue frog?

In 1891, a carnival ride opened in Atlantic City called the Observation Roundabout. A wooden wheel approximately 50 feet high with bucket-like seats attached to the structure. The roundabout elevated riders far above the ground below to a lofty perch were they witnessed the world from a new and delightful perspective. Even at a nickel a ride (which was a lot of money then) men and women lined up for a spin on the pleasure wheel. The roundabout quickly became one of the most popular rides on the Boardwalk.

William Somer was the inventor of the Observation Roundabout, and some believe his pleasure wheel inspired the Chicago Wheel at the 1893 World's Columbian Exposition in Chicago. Designed and built by George W. Ferris, Jr., the 264-foot tall structure was meant to be the beacon for the Chicago World's Fair. It succeeded! The Ferris Wheel was the Exposition's most poplar attraction and an engineering marvel.

William Somer held a patent on the design of the Observation Roundabout and later attempted to sue George Ferris for patent infringement. Mr. Somer lost, but to this day he remains a treasured son of Atlantic City's boardwalk fame and the Ferris Wheel a mainstay on the midway.

OBSERVATION ROUNDABOUT

In the darkness of night,
the colored lights of the carnival rides light up the sky.
Would you like to go on a ride like this?
What could you see from the seat on top?
What is your favorite ride at the carnival?

The family of gourds, of which pumpkins are a member, are plants that were specifically domesticated for their wide range of use. From their seed to their rinds, gourds are an important source of food for both humans and animals. When hallowed out, gourds can be crafted into a variety of utensils, vessels, musical instruments, birdhouses and objects of art.

Used in rituals and ceremonies, gourds take on the role of protector against all that is most mischievous, even evil, in the darkness of night. How better to chase evil spirits away than to scrape out a pumpkin, carve a sinister face into its rind and illuminate the cavernous eyes and fiendish mouth with a small candle. A menacing visage flickering in the wind? Scary indeed.

Defined as a fruit, pumpkins are berries and rely on honey bees for pollination. With bee populations in severe decline due to pesticides and dwindling natural habitat that provides a diversity of food for bees, some farmers are resorting to hand pollination, a labor-intensive practice that's not as reliable as Mother Nature. Pumpkins are fun and easy to grow in a home garden. Just stay away from nasty pesticides so the bees can thrive and do their work.

PUMPKIN PATCH

In the darkness of night,
jack-o-lantern faces glow, lit from within by candle light.
Do you like to carve a scary face
or a funny face into your pumpkin?
Do you dress up and go out on Halloween?

Moonbows are rare and much harder to see in comparison to their daylight twin, the rainbow. Both are of the same formation; an arc of light scattered inside water droplets, shinning outward in a spectrum of color. These miniature prisms are lit by the moon's reflected light and can only be seen under very specific weather and lunar conditions. Some people confuse the colored circle or hazy halo around the moon as a moonbow, but they are not the same.

Moonbows have fascinated man throughout history. Aristotle wrote of moonbows in 340 B.C., Mark Twain delighted in them while visiting Hawaii and John Muir witnessed them at Yosemite Falls, dubbing them "lunar spraybows".

There are several places in the world, mostly waterfalls, where this phenomenon occurs more regularly, but they can also be seen at Kilauea, the most active volcano on the Big Island of Hawaii.

MOONBOWS

In the darkness of night,
rain drops and moonlight meet to create moonbows in the sky.
Did you know you can see rainbows in the dark?
They are called moonbows.
How many colors do you see in the moonbow?

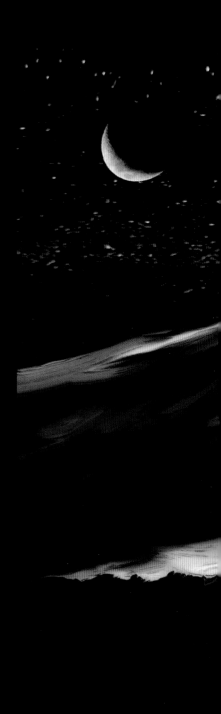

Built in 240 B.C., the Lighthouse at Alexandria on the island of Pharos was the tallest man made structure on earth. It was also the first known lighthouse and one of the Seven Wonders of the World. During the day, mirrors reflected the suns rays and at night the lamp was lit by an open fire that guided sailors safely into the harbor.

Lighthouses are found all over the world and while the mechanism of illumination has changed, the purpose of the beacon remains constant. Over the centuries the "lamp" - the term for the source of light - has been lit by various means, including wood fire, candles, electricity, and solar power. Lighthouses denote entry to a harbor and aid sailors in navigating treacherous coastlines, reefs and shoals. The use of color or painted patterns (day mark) and frequency of the lamp's flash (its night signature) indicate the lighthouse's geographic location. These distinct markings and flashes assist not only the ships' passage, but aerial navigation as well.

With advanced technology, the need for lighthouses has dimmed. Still they remain a vital navigation tool. Lighthouses have a rich history and organizations throughout the world work to preserve the legacy of these beautiful and historical landmarks.

LIGHTHOUSE

In the darkness of night,
a bright light pulses to help ships navigate
their way safely home. Have you ever seen a lighthouse?
Can you think of lights that help you find your way home?

During solar storms, huge gusts of gas and high-energy particles erupting on the suns surface are expelled into the cosmos. Once ejected from the solar atmosphere, these magnetic storms hurl through space at speeds of a million miles per hour. Most coronal mass ejections, as they are called, dissipate into the space. But on occasion they will find their way to Earth, attracted to our planet's own magnetic poles and when these storms collide with earth's atmosphere, polar auroras are created.

Science has helped us to understand these natural phenomena but our ancestors found them to be equally terrifying and wonderfully magical. Some Indian cultures believed the light and movement of the aurora was caused by their ancestor's spirits dancing. In Chinese folklore, a huge dragon flew through the night sky carrying a lighted torch in its mouth. Other cultures, frightened by the unexplained lights, believed it was a sign of evil spirits bringing war and famine. Still others rejoiced at the good fortune the light show might bring.

NORTHERN LIGHTS

In the darkness of night,
the colors of the northern lights leap and dance in the sky.
Do you live in a place where you can see the auroras?
Have you ever slept outside in a tent?
Do you think the dog in the picture gets to sleep in the tent, too?

When an object blocks the path of light, a shadow is formed. Many factors determine the shape of a shadow, including the light's source, the length and angle of light, the size of the object, and its distance from the light source. The shapes that shadows form create depth and dimension, contrast, shades of color, changes in hues and tones, definition and animation. Shadows take shape in our imagination and sometimes shadows scare us, but without them the world would seem flat, without shape or form.

Using our hands to cast shadow-animals on the wall is common bedtime play but it is considered to be one of the earliest forms of puppetry and animation. Shadow theater has been around for thousands of years, used to act out fairy tales and myths, as an aide in teaching history and a method of reporting on events that were happening in distant lands. In many cultures, Shadow Theaters are still very popular, preserving the ancient art of shadow play as a form of entertainment and education.

When was the last time you used light to make shadows?

SHADOWS

In the darkness of night,
shadows grow and change shapes.
What shadows do you see at night?
What casts silly or scary shadows at night in your house?

The Big Dipper is one of the most recognized asterisms, or star clusters, found in the night sky. The seven luminous stars that shape the Big Dipper form the body and tail of the constellation Ursa Major, the Great Bear. Because the Big Dipper is easily recognized and a constant in the night sky, it became the inspiration for many legends and myths, fueling our ancestors imaginations.

But the stars serve a practical purpose as well. Mapping the stars as a way to navigate the land, the seas, and the seasons, is an ancient practice. Farmers noted the position of the Big Dipper as a guide to the changing seasons. Sailors use them to chart their course and relied on the seven stars of the asterism to help locate true north. During the time of the Underground Railroad, runaway slaves learned a song about the drinking gourd, another name for the Big Dipper, which taught them to keep those stars in front of them as they sought passage to the north and the hope of freedom.

Locating the Big Dipper is fairly simple, especially if you consider the seasons. In fall and winter you can see it low in the sky and along the horizon; in spring and summer the stars are perched high in the night sky. Remember: spring up, fall down.

BIG DIPPER

In the darkness of night,
starlight and moonlight share the sky.
How many stars can you count in the Big Dipper?
Did you know you could get a star named after you?

The most common fireflies are nocturnal and belong to the family of winged beetles. Also known as glowworms and lightening bugs, they like warmth and moisture and are often found in marshes, along river banks or in wet, wooded areas.

The light that fireflies emit is produced by a chemical reaction called bioluminescence. The insects' light attracts mates but also provide a measure of safety, acting as a warning signal to ward off certain predators looking for something to eat. The fireflies' light can be yellow, green or pale red. It may be a steady light or intermittent, flashing on and off.

If you have fireflies, you can help them in their nighttime journey by turning off the porch lights and garden lights so the fireflies can find each other in the dark!

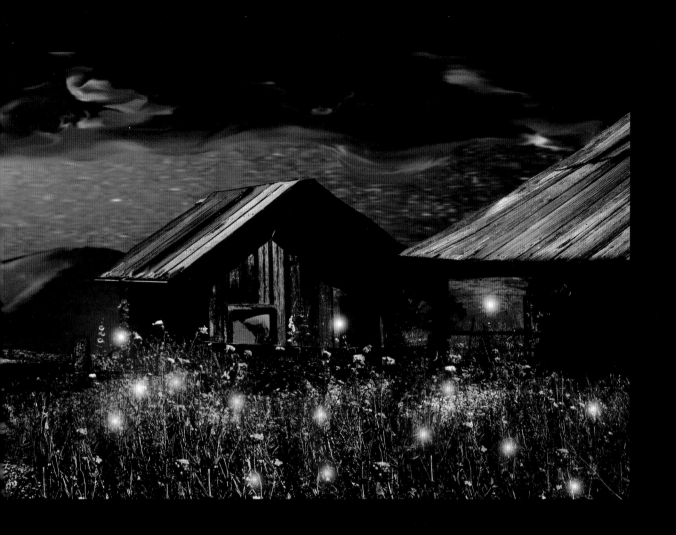

FIREFLIES

In the darkness of night,
glowworms float and flicker in the warm summer sky.
Do you have fireflies where you live?
Some people call them lightening bugs.
What other animals and insects come out at night?

The first hot air balloon was launched in 1893 carrying a sheep, a duck, and a chicken. They floated around for about 15 minutes before landing safely. About two months later, the first human ascended in a balloon. Their flight lasted about 20 minutes followed by a successful landing.

The hot air balloon, an aircraft called an aerostat, was the first vehicle in which humans flew. The first aerial photograph was taken from a hot air balloon by Felix Nadar, who went on to build an enormous balloon named Le Geant that inspired Jules Verne's novel *Five Weeks in a Balloon*. Hot air balloons also inspired adventurers who sought to make and break records flying balloons over mountains and oceans, across the earth, and into the stratosphere.

The Dawn Patrol made its first appearance in 1978 at the annual Balloon Fiesta in Albuquerque, New Mexico. Three balloons and their pilots took off an hour before dawn, illuminated by the flames that heat the air inside the balloons and allow it to rise afloat. This was the first night flight of a hot air balloon and so spectacular the sight of these buoyant balls of light rising into the predawn sky that Dawn Patrols are now a much-loved feature of balloon festivals worldwide.

DAWN PATROL

In the darkness of night,
hot air balloons float above the earth.
The bright orbs light glow in the sky before the sun rises.
Have you ever seen a hot air balloon? Would you like to take a ride in one?

The moon's light is one of the ways nocturnal moths are able to navigate the night. It serves as a reference point that helps a moth determine where it is and where it is going. Nocturnal moths are phototrophic; they are light seekers. Light helps guide their way and can also indicate a food source, dictate sleep, or warn of danger.

Light can be a source of confusion for these night travelers. Why moths flutter around a porch light or dance mad circles around a flame is still a curiosity. These lights offer no food, safety nor guidance, yet moths seem drawn to them. Some speculate that because these lights are closer and much brighter than the moon's light, they are distracting. The moths become disoriented and confused and instead of following the straight path of the moon, they seem to lose their way. Others suggest moths may mistake bright lights for sunshine and thinking it is daytime, they seek a place to hide and end up going to sleep.

Night-blooming flowers are often white and reflect light, alerting moths to a source of nectar. Perhaps the brightness of fires and man-made light excites the moths into thinking they have found a giant midnight buffet? We may never know the exact reason why moths are drawn to artificial lights. However, using yellow lights outdoors, a color moths do not respond to, can help keep the moths on their night time journey.

NOCTURNAL MOTHS

In the darkness of night,
moths take flight seeking flowers
that only open in the light of the moon.
Did you know that moths and butterflies are from the same family?
What makes them alike? What makes them different?

Most owls are nocturnal. But some, like the burrowing owl, are crepuscular - meaning that they are active in twilight hours as well as in the night. Insects that are lively at dusk and dawn are part of the diet of these small, long-legged owls which is why you might see them perched on a rock or post watching for their next meal to flit by. At night the owls hunt for rodents, their long legs allowing them to scurry and scamper across the ground in pursuit of prey.

What is most unique about this species of owl is its nesting habits. It seeks out empty burrows created by other animals but can also dig out its own shallow, underground nest. The owls line their nests with a variety of materials and sometimes collect animal dung, spreading it around the entrance to the nest to attract beetles for food.

Burrowing owls are endangered and threatened in most of their range, in large part due to human activity and the destruction of their natural habitat.

Who doesn't love a pyrotechnic celebration like the 4th of July? And we have the noisy little firecracker to thank for it. Introduced over 2,000 years ago, the explosive sound of the firecracker was said to frighten away evil spirits. The noisemakers took on an important role in most festivities, chasing away any lingering bad energy and ensuring happiness for the future.

As fireworks evolved, the design and display became more elaborate. The visual effects of fireworks became an art form as colors were added and methods of propelling the miniature rockets skyward improved. The Italians were fascinated by fireworks and made significant changes to the carrier device that launched them higher into the sky than ever before. They devised intricate designs with timed bursts of colored sparks whose points of light, called stars, trickled down from the sky in a rain of glitter. Italian firework makers also created other special effects like sparkling eruptions in the shape of fountains for the massive ground displays that were very popular in the late 1800s.

Early handlers of fireworks covered themselves in mud and fresh leaves to protect their skin from the sparks, acquiring the nickname Green Men. Modern pyrotechnics use more elaborate protective gear but are still called Green Men. Fireworks are extremely dangerous and require special training for their development, storage and use. Several professional and amateur groups teach members the art of fireworks display as well as fireworks safety.

FIREWORKS

In the darkness of night,
fireworks burst into the sky, a bright display of color and light.
Have you seen fireworks before? Did the noise of the fireworks scare you? How many
colors did you see and which ones were your favorites?

Printed in China